THE ADVENTURES OF "CHUCK E. BEAVER" AND FRIENDS

THE BIRTHDAY PARTY

Written by
Kiki

Illustrated by
SOUSOU YERETSIAN

Published by
Montbec Inc.

Publisher
MATT ARENY

Publication Advisor
JOSE AZEVEDO

Editorial Supervisor
ETHEL SALTZMAN

Artwork Supervisor
PIERRE RENAUD

ISBN 2-89227-223-8

THE BIRTHDAY PARTY

It would soon be Chuck E.'s seventh birthday, and Mr. and Mrs. Beaver were planning a very special birthday party for him. It was going to be a surprise party. All of Chuck E.'s friends had been invited, along with their parents. They all knew what time they had to be at Chuck E.'s house. No one was supposed to mention anything to Chuck E. about the party. Bobby Bear found this very hard to do.

The birthday party was set for Sunday at two o'clock in the afternoon. Everyone was told to be at Chuck E.'s house by one-thirty so that they would be there well before Chuck E. arrived. The parents were instructed to leave their cars down the road, so that Chuck E. wouldn't suspect anything as he approached the house.

Mrs. Beaver had thought of everything. She had ordered a big cake from the bakery and was planning to decorate the house in the morning, while Chuck E. and his father were out at the park.

Mr. Beaver had planned to take Chuck E. to the park to fly his new kite from noon until two o'clock. This would allow everyone plenty of time to get to the house before they got back.

On Saturday, the day before Chuck E.'s birthday, the gang had planned to go swimming together down at the local pool. Chuck E. was very excited by now, thinking about his birthday and the present his parents would give him.

"Say, Chuck E.," Bobby shouted as they splashed in the pool, "what do you think your mom and dad are getting you for your birthday?"

"Gee, I don't know, Bobby," Chuck E. answered. "This year they haven't mentioned anything. I'm wondering if they forgot all about it."

"Oh, I wouldn't worry about that," Bobby said, chuckling to himself. "Your parents would never forget your birthday."

"Bobby, do you know something I don't?" Chuck E. tried to get Bobby to talk.

"N-N-No, Chuck E.," Bobby stammered. "What makes you think that?" he asked.

"I know you, Bobby, and I can always tell when you're trying to hide something from me," Chuck E. replied.

14

"I promise, Chuck E! I'm not trying to cover anything up!" Bobby attempted to convince Chuck E. Chuck E. thought for a minute, trying to figure out how he could get Bobby to tell him what his secret was. Then it came to him.

"Say, Bobby, would you like to join me tomorrow at the park to help me fly my new kite?" Chuck E. asked.

"I can't, Chuck E.," Bobby replied without really thinking. "My parents and I were invited to go over to your house for a party."

"Ah-ha!" Chuck E. shouted. "So that's it! A surprise birthday party! Wow!"

"Oh, Chuck E., you tricked me!" Bobby said, looking very upset that he had told Chuck E. the secret. "You've got to promise not to tell your parents about this. I'll be in big trouble if they find out I told you."

"Oh, don't worry, Bobby," Chuck E. assured him. "I'll act as if I don't know anything about it! A surprise birthday party for me? This is going to be great!"

After the gang finished their swim, they all headed back home for dinner. Chuck E. and his family were sitting around the dinner table, enjoying their meal, when the phone rang.

"I'll get it, Mom!" Chuck E. volunteered, and he quickly dashed into the kitchen before anyone else could get up.

"Hello, this is the Beaver household," Chuck E. said, as he picked up the receiver.

"Hello. This is the Little Forest Bakery calling," the voice on the other end said. "Is your mother home?"

"Yes, just a minute," Chuck E. replied as he smiled to himself, thinking about a big, luscious birthday cake. He came back into the dining room to tell his mother who was on the phone.

"Mom, it's for you," Chuck E. said as he sat back down at the table. "It's the bakery calling!"

"Oh, oh, right!" Mrs. Beaver said in surprise.

While Mrs. Beaver headed into the kitchen to answer the phone, Mr. Beaver tried to look like nothing was going on. But Chuck E. knew better.

Mrs. Beaver came back into the dining room.

"Mom, what did the bakery want?" Chuck E. asked her, trying to dig a little deeper into the big secret.

"Oh, nothing important, son," Mrs. Beaver answered calmly. "They just wanted to let me know that they would be having a sale on bread next week."

"Oh, I see," Chuck E. said innocently. "Say, mom, do you know what day it is tomorrow?" he added, trying to get his mother to say something about the party.

"Well, let's see," Mr. Beaver interrupted. "Say, isn't it your birthday tomorrow?" he asked Chuck E., pretending to be surprised at his discovery.

"You know, I think you're right, dear!" Mrs. Beaver played along. "It completely slipped my mind this year. Maybe we can all go out on Monday and get you a present, son."

"Sure, Mom, that would be just fine!" Chuck E. agreed.

"Well, I can still make you a nice dinner tomorrow to celebrate your birthday," Mrs. Beaver suggested. "I hope you're not too disappointed."

"No, Mom, not at all," Chuck E. assured his mother. He smiled to himself. "It'll be a great day anyway!"

"You bet, son! We can still go down to the park and launch that new kite of yours, right?" Mr. Beaver reminded Chuck E.

"Right, Pop!" Chuck E. replied enthusiastically.

Chuck E. went to bed that night, but he couldn't fall asleep for a long time. He was thinking about what was going to happen the next day.

The next morning, Chuck E. was up very early. His baby sister Bonnie was also awake, and Mr. and Mrs. Beaver soon got up too. After a big breakfast, Mr. Beaver took Chuck E. down to the park to help him fly his new kite, as he had promised. On the way to the park, Chuck E. couldn't stop thinking about the surprise party. Finally, he couldn't hold it in any longer, so he decided to tell his father what he knew.

"Dad, I've got something to confess," Chuck E. announced. "I know all about the surprise party you and Mom have planned for me this afternoon."

"What surprise party, son?" Mr. Beaver asked, pretending not to know anything about it.

"Oh, Pop, you don't have to pretend anymore!" Chuck E. said. "Bobby told me all about it, but it wasn't his fault."

"I don't know what you're talking about, son," Mr. Beaver insisted. "Your mom and I really didn't remember your birthday until last night, so we don't know anything about a surprise birthday party."

"You mean there isn't going to be any surprise party?" Chuck E. asked, looking very dejected.

"No, son, I'm sorry but there isn't going to be any party."

"Why would Bobby lie to me about there being a surprise party, Dad?" Chuck E. kept trying to understand.

"I don't know, son, but sometimes friends like to play jokes on one another," Mr. Beaver told him. "Maybe Bobby was just trying to play a joke on you."

"Well, that's mean!" Chuck E. stammered in anger. "Wait till I see him tomorrow at school!"

"Now, son, I'm sure he didn't mean to hurt you," Mr. Beaver said, trying to calm Chuck E. down. "Why don't you just try and forget about it, and let's have a nice day, okay?"

"Oh, okay, Pop," Chuck E. agreed. "Why should I let Bobby ruin my birthday?"

"I have an idea," Mr. Beaver continued. "Why don't we go over to Bobby's house right now and ask him to join us?" he suggested.

"Yeah, that's a good idea, Pop!" Chuck E. replied. "Maybe he'll be able to explain all about the surprise party."

Mr. Beaver continued along the road to Bobby's house to see if Bobby would like to play in the park with Chuck E. and him. After he parked the car in front of Bobby's house, Mr. Beaver suggested Chuck E. go up and ask him if he wanted to join them.

"Okay, Pop," Chuck E. agreed. He knocked on Bobby's door and within a few seconds Mrs. Bear opened it.

"Oh, hi, Chuck E!" Mrs. Bear said. "What brings you here today?" she asked.

"Is Bobby home?" Chuck E. asked politely.

"Yes, he is. Would you like to go in and see him?" Mrs. Bear suggested. "He's in the living room."

"Thanks!" Chuck E. said. When he
came into the room all of his friends and
their parents suddenly jumped out from
behind the furniture and yelled, "HAPPY
BIRTHDAY, CHUCK E!"

Chuck E. was so surprised he nearly fell down. There was a real surprise birthday party after all. They had tricked Chuck E. into believing it was at his house when it was really at Bobby's.

After everyone wished him a happy birthday, Chuck E. made his way over to where Bobby was sitting.

"Hey, Bobby, I thought you told me the party was going to be at my house." Chuck E. tried to get Bobby to tell him the truth.

"It was until I told you," Bobby admitted. "After that, we had to change all the plans to keep it a secret."

"Oh, I see! My father had convinced me that there wasn't going to be any party, but I see now that he was just trying to cover up the new plans."

"Yeah, I know!" Bobby chuckled. "It was the only way to keep it a surprise."

"Do you forgive me for lying, son?" Mr. Beaver asked, as he approached Chuck E. and Bobby.

"You bet, Pop!" Chuck E. exclaimed as he hugged his father. "This is the best birthday party I've ever had!"

Just then Mrs. Beaver came into the room with a big birthday cake all aglow with lighted candles. She started everyone singing, "Happy Birthday to you! Happy Birthday to you! Happy Birthday, dear Chuck E! Happy Birthday to you!"

After everyone finished singing, Chuck E. made a wish and blew all of the candles out with one blow. Everyone clapped, and then they gave Chuck E. the presents that they had brought with them.

While Chuck E. was busy opening up his presents, he turned to see his mom and dad standing together and smiling at him.

"Thanks, Mom! Thanks, Dad!" Chuck E. said lovingly. "You've made me the happiest guy in the world today!"

Chuck E. had a wonderful birthday. Though he would have many more in the years ahead, none of them was as dear and as memorable as this one.

A birthday party's special

When your friends are all around.

To share your cake and bring you gifts

And let "Happy Birthday" sound.

                              Your friend,

                              Chuck E.